KAL YUG™

KAL YUG™

Samuel J. Narayan

Also by Samuel J. Narayan

Mortazarro: Opera of Madness
Mortazarro: The Opera Game
Mortazarro: Ungodly Realms
Age of Kali: Reflections of Death
Age of Kali: Kalidasa Games
Outlaws of the Dead: Jonah's Story

Kalibangan District 19, Aryan Empire, Apuna Coliseum, Near the Great Wall of Aryana

The first attack sent the head flying into the stands. There was a sudden roar of excitement as the well-fed citizens of Aryana toppled over one another to catch the soaring head for their personal collections, or for bragging rights, or to simply sell to the Kalidasa, the beloved designers of Kalima, the empire's preferred designer drug as the drug required the brain fluids of the dead to give users an opportunity to experience the death memories of another human being without much danger to themselves. Kalima was now the latest fad, the ultimate escape and deterrent of what many academics were calling 'positive evil' which the same academics defined as evil done in the name of boredom. Taking his eyes off the mortal combat in the blood-drenched field below, where untouchables and outlaws fought one another with the empire's latest melee weapons and technology, Jivan Rai turned toward the stands, and watched a father ram his way through the crowd. The father desperately pushed and pulled other fathers and children out of his way to catch the head. One boy nearly caught the head in mid-air, but a heavy-set citizen pushed him out of the way and the head missed his fingers and landed with a heavy thump and rolled down the concrete aisle. Dozens of citizens jumped over the fleshy trophy as though it were the last glass of water in the empire. After a great scuffle the frantic father erupted from the crowd with a victorious scream holding the severed head with a fist full of hair, an arm dripping gore, and quivering lips screaming that the head was his. A moment later he thrust the head upward and held it up proudly so all could see. The eyes of the head stared sightlessly into the coliseum and mirrored a bloodthirsty crowd as thousands laughed and roared with joy, each one wishing they had caught the head. The father waved the head around triumphantly and for a moment he stopped as though to face Jivan. Jivan could see the tattoo on the right side of the face, the tattoo that branded the original owner of the head a slave of the Brahman caste. Brahmans were the lowest of the low castes even though outlaws claimed it had never been this way and that they had once been, a long time ago, the purest of the castes at the very top of what the Athmans called the Divine Society. Many even claimed that the Athman caste had never even existed, and that the Athmans were actually the corporate elite of the old world who had hijacked and rewritten history and religion to suite their interests. It wouldn't have surprised him. And he didn't care. That's the way history worked. Today the elite, tomorrow the oppressed. Today the rebel, tomorrow the tyrant. He stared at the tattoo, then the eyes, and the eyes stared back at him. He didn't feel anything, not an ounce of pity. Not for this slave turned outlaw. If he did feel anything at all it was something more akin to pleasure. He felt pleased. Deeply pleased. One less outlaw in the world. The world was a better place. If not the world, at least the empire.

Suddenly a buzz noise echoed through the coliseum. A head-sized tele-orb hovered and sailed in to capture the father's gushing joy. On all the big screens in the coliseum, the father showed the empire the Brahman's head and the empty dead eyes stared at the citizens of Aryana and the citizens—whose brutality, bloodlust and boredom knew no bounds by day or night—cheered gloriously and were all envious that this man, this proud father, would be taking home an outlaw head. One day, they all wished, they too would catch a soaring outlaw head. At that moment the father kneeled to lift his excited seven-year-old son in his free arm. Then he placed the head in the boy's hands and the boy lifted it by the hair and shook it once more, emulating his father. At once the hovering orb moved in for a close up. An emotional moment between father and son. This was what it was all about. Coming to the games with your children. Sharing a moment. Bonding. After a few seconds the tele-orb cut to a commercial about a band of outlaws trying to destroy the Great Wall; Jivan knew it was a lie: fabricated news to keep citizens in a state of constant fear and distraction, and he quickly returned his attention to the carnage below where two teams of gladiators battled one another with gleaming bronze vibro-swords and spears over a slippery ground strewn with heads, limbs, and dark deathly fluids.

Jivan was part of this 'keeping citizens in a state of constant fear.' And he loved his job. Everyone, he thought, should be paid to do what they loved. He watched the fight below with curiosity. There were only two men on one team left, and five on the other. Even from where he stood, he could see the blood and sweat dripping off the bronze armor and leather pads. He could sense the presence and excitement of death. Then, to his surprise, he felt a slight surge of adrenalin, when one gladiator lifted his bronze vibro-sword and rammed the electrified blade through the helmet of his enemy and dashed out flesh, blood and brains, evening out the odds. Within seconds it was four against two. The gladiator pulled the dripping sword out of the helmet and the body collapsed to the ground. It was an impressive maneuver, which replayed on the tele-screens above, but his victory was short-lived. Just as he turned he received a long bronze spear through the neck. At once the gladiator grabbed the spear with one hand and lifted his sword with the other. He severed the spear to free himself, then he rushed toward the gladiator who had punctured his throat. With his last breath he vaulted and plunged his sword between the gladiator's eyes. The dull blade instantly crushed the skull, and both eyes burst out of the socket adding to the senseless gore on the ground. Then the gladiator, with a throat full of blood and bronze, attempting to yank out the spear, managed to pull out half his throat with the effort and fell with a terrible gurgle. He groveled and writhed like a dying fish on the ground and the orb rushed in for a close up. Within mere moments it was three against one, and Jivan noticed that the crowd applauded emotionlessly, and he instantly sensed the games were starting to lose their effect.

Everywhere he turned it was the same. Bullshit and violence. It was what citizens needed. It was what citizens wanted. It was an ancient formula of control, almost as ancient as Rome or the countless forgotten civilizations that came before Rome. He stared below at three men trying to eliminate one and felt a slight surge of excitement. The rules were team deathmatch that would end in straight elimination. Two teams fought to the death. When one was completely eliminated it became free-for-all. Only one could survive. But none usually did. Wounds were often mortal. Even if the gladiator survived to fight another day, he usually didn't. He usually died in his cell, or if he survived to fight another game he was used as bait for one of the opening acts that featured corporate advancements in gene weaponry; in other words, the empire's latest monstrosities—genetic chimeras that were made just for the entertainment of Aryan citizens. Now the Deadlands were filled with these wandering creatures like dinosaurs that were referred to by the media as the Chimerik. Failed mutations and coliseum wonders that citizens usually got bored with after one or two games. They were disposed of outside of the Great Wall and sometimes they weren't even killed or incinerated. Without realizing that these test tube mutations could potentially find a way to reproduce, the Deadlands were now infested with all sorts Chimeriks that some believed would one day be the end of humanity. Jivan didn't think so. He was sure that humanity would be the end of humanity and that all that would remain of humanity would be the Chimerik. As scientists made Chimeriks stronger and stronger, fiercer and fiercer to appease low attention spans, and as these scientists attempted to outdo one another for the games, they would one day create a creature that would turn on its creator and herald in the next dinosaur age. This was certainly possible. Often Jivan wondered if a forgotten scientifically advanced civilization was responsible for the first dinosaur age. Maybe a civilization like their own experimented the way they did with gene and andro technology for their curiosity and entertainment. And maybe, just maybe nuclear war or plague wiped out this civilization out and the only creatures that survived were the genetic mutations they had created. Creatures history remembered as dinosaurs. It was certainly a possibility. If it could happen now it could certainly have happened thousands of years ago. After the Collapse, after the Great Wars and the Purge and all the bio-weapons that were created for the sole purpose of man's destruction nothing would have surprised Jivan. Nothing. And he did believe the cliché: history repeated itself. It always did. To Jivan, Aryana was nothing more than the oppression and brutality of Rome and the rumored science and technology of Atlantis all rolled in one. Jivan shifted in his seat and watched the gladiators swing great vibro-swords at on another. Unlike the majority of citizens, Jivan was lean and fit; his physique was more of a battle-hardened general than a soft-bellied Aryan. Even before andro technology had replaced most of his human parts, he had been this way. He was and always had been an incarnation of raw wolfish power. Only now Aryan technology had made him harder, stronger, stealthier, one of the Empire's best agents. His face was deeply scared, his head was shaved, his eyes were glistening black pearls, and beneath his urban uniform—consisting of a thin bullet-proof leather jacket and black jeans—were the machinations of Aryan ingenuity. Machinations that reminded him every moment of every day about his undying hate for those who had robbed him of his former life. There was a sense of purpose fueled by hate about him. And he had a purpose. And he did hate. And he would exterminate every last outlaw like rats before he issued his last breath. It was a promise he made himself every night before he slept—if he slept at all. Technology made it so he only need one or two hours of sleep a night. Memories made it so he got even less.

Now Jivan turned to the crowd at the lower levels. He could see that these citizens weren't even enjoying the games. They were waiting. They were eagerly waiting for the games to be over so that they could rush the field and harvest heads for their collections, or to sell to the Kalidasa for Kalima. When the Games first started years ago, the Athmans didn't really want citizens rushing the fields. But they soon realized that the battles between citizens for gladiator heads was often more entertaining than the games themselves. So they permitted the 'rush' and they let the cameras roll. They even sold lower-level seats at a premium. The Athmans, however, had made it clear that citizens were no longer bound to the laws of the empire or the Divine Society once they willingly entered a coliseum contaminated with low caste blood. And Jivan agreed with his Athman masters. It was definitely more entertaining to watch these well-fed citizens fight one another for heads and bragging rights than to watch the gladiators go at it.

Suddenly Jivan heard a slight ring echo in his mind. He instantly sent a thought-impulse to answer his Satellite-Interface, or S-I, as it was usually termed. A second later an image only he could see appeared before him. It was his handler, Zaraz Keel.

"Evening Ji," he said. "Hope I'm not interrupting anything too important, but something urgent has come up."

It must have been urgent or else he wouldn't have called him so late in the evening. "I'm listening." Jivan whispered.

"I know this is last minute, but we need to create a piece to divert the masses from the death of Kulwar Singh. Kulwar was murdered this morning in his home, and we suspect Sundri and her band of outlaws." Definitely not good. Kulwar Patwa Singh Gill was the empire's hero turned reality-tv actor. The thought that he had been assassinated in the comfort of his own home would undermine Athman-Aryan superiority. Zaraz continued:

"As you know Kulwar produced one of the Empire's most popular reality shows. On it he and his officers hunted down outlaws in the Deadlands to showcase the Empire's newest weapons and technology. A few weeks ago he had hunted down and killed some of Sundri's men. Those he captured alive he tortured for hours, later he sold the Kalima at a premium at his website. We think it was more than Sundri could bear, and that she herself infiltrated the empire to eliminate him."

"Go on."

"If it were to get out that Outlaws succeeded at infiltrating the Empire to assassinate our esteemed hero, many Athmans would lose face.

"Not good."

"No. Not good. We will be announcing his death tomorrow morning as heart failure, and we need a strong piece to distract citizens from poking their noses into this."

Jivan figured as much. This was what his team was created for. Staging events, manipulating opinion, distracting—advanced psy-ops.

Biopixels materialized, a picture appeared and blocked the games below. To all others it seemed as though Jivan was watching the games and mumbling to himself when he answered Zaraz.

"Take a look at this picture." Zaraz said. A picture of a man in a white neeta appeared before Jivan. He was clearly an Athman. Only Athmans were allowed to wear the pristine white neetas as a symbol of their purity.

"Recognize him?"

"Should I?"

"This man, Jacob Varma, is a powerful lawyer and suspected sympathizer for untouchables. We suspect he is also part of a nefarious underground train to help runaway slaves escape the Empire."

Jivan snickered. He and his team had been trying to break the train movement for years now, and it seemed as though every time he destroyed one 'train' another sprang up. Zaraz continued:

"Your assignment is to find out who he's working with and to make him tomorrow morning's public enemy number one."

"Shouldn't be too difficult."

"Careful, Ji. The last time you said that you nearly blew the division."

"Didn't have the right intel. Wasn't my fault."

"Just take extra precautions. The last thing we want is citizens questioning what we tell them."

"Understood."

The S-I faded out, and soon Jivan was watching the last two surviving gladiators exchange death blows. With one swipe of a sword, one gladiator let loose a bloodcurdling cry as a blade sliced his belly open. His sword fell to the hard, dirt ground. He crumbled to his knees with a smiling gash in his belly from left to right. He instinctively tried to prevent his innards from spilling out without success. As the gladiator issued his last breath and toppled over another fallen gladiator the crowd went mad. Not even a second later the lower-level rushed the coliseum arena and fought one another for gladiator heads as the surviving gladiator was escorted back to his cell. Jivan chuckled. It was fun. It was entertaining, but not that fun, not that entertaining—not anymore. He had to admit he was starting feel that it was getting old. The whole affair with the end game 'rush' was getting tedious and repetitive. Soon it wouldn't be enough. Soon the Athmans would have to come up with a new show, a new game, or maybe just new rules to keep things interesting. To keep citizens out of their affairs. Jivan laughed to himself. He loved all this entertainment and distraction. He loved history and the things history inspired. Old formula, he thought. Old formula, but good formula. Effective formula. Probably the reason it was still being used in new and exciting ways. He couldn't wait to see what the Athmans would come up with next week. He should reserve his tickets. Agents got special discounts

Kamboja District 13, The Projects

Later that night Jivan drove his black t-rax through the dark recesses of the empire searching for one of his most trusted connections to the underworld—Chiron. Chiron and Jivan had been working together for a little over a year now. Jivan helped Chiron stay out of jail, and Chiron helped Jivan put his competition in jail. The relationship was symbiotic to say the least. On the street Chiron was known as the go-to guy for illegal Kalima, death experiences that were censored by the empire for being in some way or another a threat to peace and stability. Dangerous memories, the Athmans called them. Usually such Kalima was made out of the death memories of the Asura Forces or the Hanuman Guard fighting out in the Deadlands against the outlaws. According to the news there were little or no casualties and the war against the outlaws was almost won. Almost. According to the news. Bullshit. Bullshit heaped on top of bullshit. The more you watched the less you knew. Old formula. Effective formulaJivan knew better. He knew that the outlaws were growing in strength and numbers. He knew that bands of outlaws were starting to organize into one single unified band and that united they would be impossible to defeat. He had heard of the leader, Sundri. He had heard she was moving from band to band uniting the divided in the Deadlands. She had to be assassinated for the sake of Aryan peace and security, and now she and her band had assassinated the one who had been charged with her assassination. Kulwar Patwa Singh Gill. Nothing could be more insulting. Nothing could be more revealing of Athman-Aryan imperfection. Citizens could not discover what had happened to their hero. It would be pandemonium in the streets. It was for reasons like these the Athmans had created the psy-ops division. To always ensure control of public knowledge and opinion. Jivan had been pulled off the Special Forces to lead this special division that did not exist and would never exist on record. He was chosen because he was the best, because he had hunted down more outlaws than any other agent, and because he essentially owed what remained of his life to the Athmans who had given him a second chance with their humanoid technology--technology that had replaced eighty percent of his body after a brutal encounter with the outlaws; an encounter that had left his entire family slaughtered.

It was fair to say Jivan loathed the outlaws, and he had devoted every atom of his being to annihilating them. So when he had been approached by Zaraz Keel to lead the deadliest agents in the empire to fight the outlaws on the psychological as well as physical front he didn't have to think twice. Now he had access to the empire's best technology and agents, some fifty or so agents whose identity only he knew as the leader of Research and Destroy. Otherwise referred to as RAD. Depending on the assignment Jivan would select his agents carefully. This assignment he didn't have to think about who he would need. It was a standard psy-ops assignment. He would need his media specialists, those agents who could help him stage the scene he would need to divert attention from the assassination of Kulwar Patwa Singh Gill. And so he had summoned agents Harun and Shera. Using his S-I, he warned them that he would need their services toward the end of the night. They chimed back in saying that they were awaiting further orders. Now Jivan spotted Chiron selling Kalima to a transmana which always sent a chill down his spine. Technology and science made anything possible in Aryana, but some things, some things like gene manipulation and surgery to sculpt your features to look more like an animal or a god was something straight out of a myth or a nightmare. Since the process had been approved by the Emperor, the streets of Aryana began to fill with people who were taking gene modifiers and undergoing operations to mold their features so that they resembled the animal or god of their choosing. Strangely enough, the only citizens who were not allowed to contaminate their genes or undergo such operations were the Athmans. Athman genes were considered pure and divine. Such meddling was banned by the Laws of Athma.

Sighing, Jivan waited for the man with strong elephant features to leave. The man argued with Chiron, and Chiron instantly pulled out an old revolver and placed it on the man's trunk-like proboscis. The man raised his thick greyish-blue hands and backed off. He cursed something unintelligible, then a moment later he was gone.

At once Jivan stepped out of his t-rax. The door hissed behind him as he marched toward his old friend. Chiron greeted him with a smile and laugh:

"Jivan Rai!"

"Chiron." Jivan grinned.

"Why is the Empire's best visiting me at this hour?" He patted Jivan's black leather jacket. "Looking for something you can't buy in stores. Kalima, perhaps. If you are, you're in luck. I have a fresh batch made from the deaths of thugees. An outfit of Asura killed them off last night in the Deadlands. Made them suffer for a long time before finally killing them. Brutal. Tragic. Everything you'd expect from a designer drug. A kid I know at the base brought me a fresh batch of death this morning, and each death, by Athma, is a real trip."

"Not looking for Kalima. Looking for something a little more devastating."

Chiron raised an eyebrow and waited. At last Jivan said:

"N7."

Chiron gave a shrill, disbelieving whistle and cocked his head. "What the fuck does the empire want with N7?"

He waited for an answer. When none came he said:

"Fine don't tell me, but N7 is unstable. Could backfire on the one using it."

"I have no intention of using it but I'll keep that in mind. Are you able to help me?"

Chiron nodded, but didn't seem too pleased. A moment later he was sending impulses and requests to one of his partners through a dated version of a Special Forces S-I Jivan had bartered with him for intel a few months ago.

Chiron shifted uneasily, and Jivan could sense he didn't want to help him on this one, and he understood his reluctance. N7 was created during the Great War—the war that followed the collapse before the Aryan Empire had been founded by some of the richest businessmen in Asia.

N7 was a weapon that didn't eliminate the enemy, rather it suspended animation so people could be captured and enslaved.

It was a blue gas that filled enclosures and froze the enemy in a block of blue ice. It was designed by one of the founding Athmans of Aryana who felt it was a waste, a real waste, to kill the enemy when the enemy could be captured, preserved and put to use for the corporation. Those times were chaotic. Corporations fighting corporations for control of the world and its resources. Several united in the east and the west to finally form the New American Republic in the West and the Aryan Empire in the East. An Armistice between the Republic and Empire was signed so that they could both contend with the outlaws in the wastelands outside the walls of empire and republic. Land they referred to as the Deadlands because life was short and brutal with the lack of laws and infrastructure of civilization. Though outlaws were spared the lies and indoctrination of the empire, they often fought one another for basic provisions. Most of the outlaws scavenging in the Deadlands had been denied citizenship for having refused to fight for any corporation during the Wars. Now they were non-citizens. Or just plain outlaws. They could still become citizens if they wanted to, but not in this life. In this life they could enter Aryana as the lowest of the low castes. After several lives of unquestionable devotion to the Aryan castes, they would, through karma eventually become Aryan-Athmans themselves.
Within minutes a cloaked man emerged from the dark alley, handed Chiron a canister, then disappeared without a word. By the frustrated expressions on Chiron's face, Jivan instantly understood they were arguing over their S-Is.

Hesitantly, Chiron handed it over shaking his head. "What are you getting yourself into?"

Jivan smiled. "I'd tell you, but—"

"You'd have to kill me," Chiron laughed, he turned around. The line was getting old. He knew Jivan had appropriated it from a film he had sold him. A film from the old world which was illegal and should have been incinerated during the Purge. Jivan enjoyed these old movies and didn't know why. These movies and books could still be salvaged beyond the Wall of the Empire in the Deadlands. Chiron didn't understand why these films and books had to be destroyed. He forgot what the Reclamation and Purge was all about. Something about chaos. Something about the divine society and getting rid of anything that might contradict or undermine Athman rule. Something about erasing anything that offered a different interpretation of history than the one the Athmans claimed. Something about the Athmans not even existing before the Great War. Chiron didn't know. He didn't want to know. He didn't care. It didn't matter. All he care about was the profit he made selling ancient books and movies. Books and movies that sold for more rupees than illegal Kalima. "I don't want to know." There were a lot of things Chiron didn't know and didn't want to know. He shook his head and walked away, disappearing into the shadows of the alley.

Jivan turned and suddenly—

Sensed a dart penetrate his humanoid mech arm.

A cloaked man commanded. "Don't move." When he saw Jivan wasn't going down, he fired another dart, and another.

Jivan pulled out one dart after another and smashed them against the ground.

"What the fuck are you!" The concealed man panicked.

Jivan pulled out the last dart and stared at the man, the dart, and then the man. "Not a person you want to be fucking with."

The man was a scavenger. Jivan could tell by the tattoo-brand on the side of his face; he was a slave, an untouchable, a low caste. He had likely escaped his master but not the Walls of the Empire. Now to survive he was disappearing citizens and selling them to Kali-Bongs, or K-Bongs as they were called.

Disgusting thing a K-Bong.

Ultimate legal manifestation of positive evil. Or so Jivan thought, but never openly. For a little money you rented a room and a human being who you could pretty much do anything you wanted to so long that human being was a low caste. Evil. Fuckin evil. But not according to the high and noble castes. The Aryans. To the Aryan castes this was their divine right.Jivan wasn't a low caste; he was a mid-caste, so he couldn't be sold to a legitimate k-bong. He surmised he was meant for an illegal k-bong. A k-bong where low castes would visit to take out their day to day frustrations on an Aryan caste member. Or maybe he wasn't meant for a k-bong. Maybe this scavenger meant to harvest his organs for doctors, or his memories for Kalima. He couldn't be sure. In a way he felt sorry for this scavenger, but not that much.

Jivan smiled. The scavenger narrowed his gaze, not understanding. Then, in a movement too fast to track, Jivan slammed the last dart into the scavenger's neck. At once the tranquilizer filled his artery, the robber staggered left, then right and finally collapsed on the hard ground. A moment later Jivan placed the N7 in the trunk of his t-rax and was hovering toward the opulent districts of Kurushara. As Jivan left one district for another, a citizen stumbled over the unconscious scavenger. He cautiously kneeled over the body and checked the face to make sure he was a low caste; when he saw the tattoo of the untouchable and the serial number, he smiled a pleased Aryan smile; an instant later he summoned one of his servants and commanded him to bring this scavenger home. The servant nodded and obeyed. He lifted the scavenger over his shoulder and followed his master who would use this unfortunate scavenger for his own fun and entertainment. His master would make him last for days, a week perhaps. This night and the next few nights his master wouldn't have to visit a k-bong. This night the gods had blessed him. They had been generous. Athma, the god of the gods, the god who inspired and oversaw all gods and religions, had heard his prayers to help him find a way to save a little bit of money. His master had just been complaining to his wife that k-bongs were getting too expensive and that soon it would be cheaper to buy a slave at the slave market than rent one at a k-bong.

Kurushara District 17, Zaro Drive

Jivan tailed Jacob to a k-bong. Which didn't make much sense to him. It didn't fit Jacob's profile even though he was an Aryan-Athman. By everything he had read in his file Jacob was against the divine hierarchy and was a known untouchable sympathizer. Then it dawned on Jivan. This was no ordinary k-bong, no ordinary temple of torture for Athman rituals. This was a stop on an undercover train. A stop where they brought runaway slaves before they continued on a path that would eventually lead under or over the Great Wall and into the Deadlands. As he surveyed the k-bong a transport hovercraft maneuvered its way to the back. For disposal, Jivan thought, and then realized what was really going on, and it all began to make sense. He hovered silently toward the k-bong to get a closer look. There in the back he saw Jacob piling bodies into the back of the transport. Jivan smiled. Of course. This wasn't just a stop on an underground train. This was the last stop. Next stop: freedom.
Instantly Jivan realized that those bodies weren't dead. They weren't dead at all. They were runaway slaves. They were going to be transported just outside the Wall to the cremation grounds where low castes and outlaws and citizens who betrayed the divine society were incinerated. He had heard of a herb or plant mixture of sorts that slowed the heart rate to such a degree that not even a scan-drone could detect life. That's how they did it. That's how they passed the gates undetected. They would escape in suspended animation and, he imagined, the driver would administer the adrenalin shot needed to be revived once free.

This train seemed a lot more complicated than all the others he had shut down over the years. Most trains always ended up in a dangerous trek leagues beneath the ground through man-made tunnels that ended up in a quarry or mine in the Deadlands. Easier trains to spot where those who had slaves climb over the Wall. These trains were the easiest to break. Climbing over the Great Wall was the easiest yet the most dangerous way out. One shot from a security drone and you were vaporized. Now they were testing new munitions that caused every cell to explode with more force than a grenade. Nothing remained. Total vaporization. The empire had tried to arm security forces with these guns, but the bullets were toxic and caused human users to slowly rot away and disintegrate after one or two weeks of use. For now, only the drones could handle this new technology. For now. Of course they were experimenting with prisoners and untouchables but it would be years before such technology was made harmless to citizens. Now and then they showcased such a weapon at a coliseum game. But they never really showed what happened to the gladiator who wielded the weapon after. Though the gladiator with the vaporizer always won the games, he had been better off shot by his own gun than experience the slow agonizing death that followed.

Jivan peered at the k-bong. He wondered if anything was going on inside. He wondered if they were actually torturing people in there. If they were, he was sure they were torturing upper castes and not low castes. He had uncovered a chain of illegal k-bongs last year. Hundreds of upper castes had been killed by slaves just wanting a little pay back. A little release from the stress of day-to-day abuse and bondage. These k-bongs had opened up in the slums and countless prominent Aryan-Athmans had been murdered there. A few had survived, but not many. Many would have been saved had they warned Athmans about what was happening to them in the news. But that never happened, and that would never happen. Nothing that undermined the divinity of the Athman caste would ever make the news. Any other caste, sure. But not the Athmans. The Athmans were living representations of Athma, and nothing could happen to them. Nothing, indeed. Jivan had been the one charged with closing these k-bongs down and retrieving all the Kalima that had been made with the death memories of these Athmans. It was incredible, he thought, how much death and entertainment science could get out of one death. He had kept a few pills, and used one or two to navigate the deaths of a few Athmans in order to find the clues he needed to end the Athman slaughter. He remembered the Kalima. The death itself wasn't as alarming or special as those committing the crime. When Athmans tortured and killed low castes there was more boredom than pleasure in the eyes. When low castes tortured and killed upper castes it was neither boredom or pleasure in the eyes but a pure red hate.

Now Jivan watched Jacob load the transport for a long while. At last Jacob got in the passenger seat and hovered away. In any other circumstance Jivan would stop these slaves from escaping. But Jacob was the bigger picture, and he needed him to return home. And so, he let Jacob free these slaves; and just as he was about to make his way to Jacob's estate, a knock on his window startled him. He looked up to see a devadas smiling at him. No ordinary devadas either. A woman who looked more like a cat than human. She smiled and winked:

"Looking to try something new." She purred.

"Go away."

"Not expensive."

"Not interested."

Jivan shook his finger at her, and then motioned her away like dirt. Instantly she lost her smile and kicked his t-rax. He winced. Not for his car, but at the insult. In any other circumstance a devadas would never get away with such an assault. But this time she or it or whatever you called it was lucky. It would live to kick another car. As she stomped away cussing and cursing, he reversed out into the lane, and made his way to Jacob's estate.

Kurushara, Aryan Prime

Jivan wasn't an Athman-Aryan, but he had a chip embedded in his wrist that gave him access to all the districts in the empire and at all times. Many called this all-access chip the green chip. Most RAD agents had green chips. Zone restrictions and curfews was one of the many ways that the Athmans kept control of low castes. Untouchables were permitted to enter Aryan districts to work during the day, but bynight they needed to be in their designated zones. Each caste had its own zone where they were assigned a small pucca dwelling and daily rations so as to be able to raise a family and continue the caste line. There were hundreds of sub-castes within the low castes, and slaves could wander from low caste zone to low caste zone for as long as they wanted but what they could not do was request a move or request a pucca in a zone that did not correspond with their caste. Intermarriages between low castes were permitted, but the family would have to live in the zone of the lower of the two castes, and the children born to mixed-castes would be born into the lowest caste of the two parents. This way Athmans ensured a steady supply of specialized slaves and Divine Society would continue in perfect peace, balance and harmony. With this almost flawless structure, every crack of dawn saw floods of slaves entering Aryan areas to do their day's work and then emptied out by noon. Only those lucky to work in home were permitted to stay in Aryan districts past noon, and they, for the most part had to stay out of sight for fear of contaminating the area with their contaminated souls. By midnight, all slaves had to leave Aryan districts. But there were exceptions.

Some Aryans were allowed live-in slaves, but those slaves had special chips implanted in them. Any untouchable caught in an Aryan district past curfew was instantly spotted by satellite and was subsequently given electroshocks through their caste chips until they had found a way to get to a legal zone. There was only one problem: sometimes the shocks stunned the untouchable unconscious so that he couldn't leave the high caste zone and was consequently electrocuted. It was the same or at least a similar technique the Athmans used to contain cattle and horses and other farm animals. As soon as they moved out of legal territory they were shocked. Animals learned fast. Slaves, faster. One of the first things a slave planning to escape had to do was get rid of his caste chip without being electrocuted in the process of removing it, for the chip had an anti-removal device that released enough electricity to electrocute an entire herd of cattle let alone one poor slave. It was a cost-effective way of keeping low castes in line with Divine Society. Slaves were usually very punctual and they almost always emptied out of Aryan zones a good fifteen minutes before their permitted time which varied on a slave-by-slave basis. For exposure to these shocks for longer than an hour often resulted in death or irreversible slave-shock. So the security orb patrolling the Aryan neighborhood was just an extra precaution against hacks. But Jivan was legit, and so when the orb hovered over his t-rax, it scanned him, beeped an unintelligible sentence, and left him without alerting the police or the Hanuman Guard.

For a long while Jivan observed Jacob's estate. It was a fifteen bedroom home with a massive perimeter wall. He wasn't that impressed. Most Athmans had much bigger homes than this. This, he thought, wasn't the home of a living God. He was just about to instinctively question Athman divinity but then stopped himself and quickly held back his thoughts for fear of being monitored. He had heard that the Athmans were working on a way to read thoughts through S-I technology. Nothing was confirmed. But he wasn't taking any chances as it was a crime to say or think anything against the Athmans.

For the longest time Athmans could only monitor what was said. Now with S-I technology it seemed as though they were getting closer and closer to a way to read, record and filter thoughts on a massive scale. Or they were already there, they already had the technology and hadn't announced their discovery to the empire. For now the idea that they could use his S-I to read his thoughts was enough even if it was just a rumor. And even though it was just a rumor he already found himself self-editing his thoughts and watching what he thought. He personally didn't think it so impossible. S-I technology seemed impossible only twenty years ago, and now if he could answer and call others with thought impulses through a brain-satellite interface then thought reading, scanning and searching was certainly in the realm of possibility. If he could communicate with thought whispers though an S-I system that relayed information and images created by the brain, why couldn't those same thoughts be hacked into. If the Kalidasa could design drugs that allowed you to relive memories of the dead through Kalima, why couldn't other memories and thoughts be harvested. It could be. It wasn't a far stretch of the imagination, and questioning Athman divinity certainly wasn't worth dying for. For any thought against the Athman caste was punishable by death by purification. Meaning, if a person was caught saying or thinking thoughts against the Atmans hot liquid led was poured into the ears in order to purify the brain of its contaminated thoughts. He had seen it done many times before. Before the coliseum games began anyone who had committed a crime against the divine caste by word or action were executed according to the Laws of Athma. Thoughts questioning the divinity of the Athmans wasn't worth the risk. He could think of so many other things. So why question Athman divinity or interpretations of the Divine Society. Jivan walked down to the gate at the front of the estate and connected his hack unit to the keypad. Within seconds the security system was disabled and he was stealthily climbing over the wall. He moved through trees and garden and found a small window. He peered inside and decided he wouldn't infiltrate through the obvious point of entry. In all likelihood there was something like a drone or trap waiting for him. So he pulled out his grapple gun, fired toward the roof, and commenced a silent climb upward. Two minutes later he was on the roof placing his grapple gun away. Creeping panther-like, in case there were guards below, he crossed the flat roof until he reached the skylight. He pulled out a metal pick and began fiddling with the lock. A click instantly signaled success. But before he infiltrated the home he closed his eyes and connected with RAD's satellite. A moment later a body heat picture appeared in his mind. He observed himself and three other in the estate. As he had suspected: Guards.

Silently, he lowered himself into the room. He made tiny imperceptible movements toward the door. He paused a moment. Then he opened the door and made his way to the guard in the security room. A moment later he pressed his ear against the door. He heard the guard reciting hymns from one of the thousand religions in the empire.

Athmans permitted anyone to create and register any cult or religion so long as they embraced Athma as the god of their god, and so long as their cult or religion did not undermine or contradict Athman-Aryan Caste Society. In this way the Athmans actually seemed a paradigm of tolerance. On the surface the Athmans appeared accepting of all. On the surface. The purge and Aryan Reclamation proved otherwise. In those dark and chaotic times anyone who believed in the old religions that blatantly refused to accept or acknowledge caste society was disappeared or exiled to the Deadlands. Hindus, Christians, Sikhs, Muslims and Jews who didn't believe in caste or Athma were simply purged. Now there were hundreds of empire-approved sects and interpretations of Hinduism, Christianity, Sikhism, Islam, and Judaism and each new interpretation embraced the god of gods, Athma, and his divine caste society. You could subscribe to any religion you wanted so long as it did not contradict divine truth as interpreted and revealed by the Athmans. In this way all religions were tolerable since they did not directly contradict or undermine Athman control; and so, Athman-Christians, Athman-Jews, Athman-Muslims, and Athman-Hindus and Athman-Sikhs ruled and controlled society without worry of rebellion or protest from the untouchables.

Jivan listened to the prayers. This guard, guessing by the scripture he was reciting, was a mid-caste Christian reciting passages from the Bible as interpreted by the Athmans. Many Christian outlaws, however, would have said rewritten and not interpreted. They maintained that Christians had never subscribed to caste, that Jesus had never been an Athman, and that these were all lies invented by the Emperor and the noble castes to maintain caste slavery and control. Most outlaws running the trains in and out of the empire were Christians. Though the most feared and fierce outlaw of them all, the outlaw who ran trains and who boldly attacked slave caravans running in and out of the empire was a Sikh. A Sikh of old named Sundri. An outlaw who swore her sword would be the end of caste slavery.

Jivan opened the door slowly. The guard had his eyes closed and was reciting a prayer without missing a beat. Jivan took two steps forward, then came down on the side of the guard's neck with a devastating blow that instantly rendered him unconscious. When he had finished gagging and cuffing him, he crept out into the hallway and closed the door behind him. One down, two more to go.

He moved slowly down the stairs to the kitchen where one guard was preparing a sandwich. He gently pulled out his silencer. He aimed. Fired. The dart penetrated the back of the fleshy neck. The guard released his sandwich and slapped his neck as though he had been bitten by a horse fly. Slowly and drowsily he turned to face Jivan. Instantly Jivan rushed up to him and caught him mid-air before he collapsed to the ground and alarmed the other guard to a potential disturbance.

Slowly and gently, Jivan released him. Two down, one to go. The basement. With soundless steps Jivan made his way down to the basement, but didn't find the guard when he got there. He shuffled back in the shadows and was just about to consult his S-I when he heard a toilet flush. The bathroom directly ahead of him. He aimed his silencer. He waited. After a moment the door slowly opened with the light of the bathroom slowly revealing Jivan…aiming…a gun. A moment later the guard stumble back, tripped over the toilet and fell with a crash into the tub.

Jivan took in a deep breath, then made his way back to the kitchen where he hefted the guard and quickly returned to the basement. He dumped him in the tub with the other guard, cuffed and gagged them, and then made his way upstairs to the living room. There he enabled the security system he had disabled and waited. Jivan didn't wait long before headlights pulled into the driveway and a hovercraft lowered gently to the ground with a soft hiss.

Jivan shuffled back and hid in the shadows next to the door. He closed his eyes and listened. The thump of footsteps, the chime of the keypad, the handle turning, the door squeaking. He opened his eyes and prepared to strike.

The thud of an unconscious body hitting the ground.

It took twenty minutes to prepare Jacob, plant the N7 in his home, and finally contact Harun and Shera. Jivan made himself some chai, and then made his way to the front door to greet his team. They walked in with their laptops and cameras. They didn't need to ask. They knew what this was about. Psy-ops. Opinion control. They were there to fabricate a story. Shera smiled at Jivan, and he nodded as she set up her cameras and waited for Jacob to come to. An hour later Jacob opened his heavy eyes to see Jivan sitting in front of him. He tried to move, but found he was cuffed, ankles and wrists to his kitchen chair. His eyes instantly darted to the table where he observed a spread of knives and tools.

Jivan smiled, reached for the table, grabbed a hammer and began slowly pounding his palm. This was the part Jivan enjoyed. This was the part he exceled at. Intimidation and interrogation. He didn't know where the skill had come from. But this was what he felt he was born to do and why he was such an asset to the empire. By Jacob's profile, he already knew Jacob would give him nothing. But he would enjoy getting nothing out of him anyway. It didn't matter. Intel wasn't his primary objective. Distraction was. Nevertheless he would try. After an oppressive silence he smiled and said:

"Jacob Varma, champion of the oppressed, do you know who I am?" Jacob didn't answer. Jivan continued. "More importantly, do you know why I'm here?" Again no answer. Jivan smiled. "I'm here, to make you famous." He nodded sincerely. "I'm here to make news. That's what we do." He motioned toward Shera behind the camera and Harun behind his laptop. Jacob squirmed in his seat. Jivan consulted his S-I and saw that Jacob was consciously trying to calm himself down.

His S-I was an indispensable tool to his interrogations especially since RAD had introduced a lie detection feature which read fluctuations in body heat, chemistry and expressions. Not that he would need it with Jacob, but still, it was brilliant. Any answer would reveal through body chemistry and emotion whether he was being lied to or not. There weren't many slaves or outlaws who could beat the S-I lie-detector. In fact, there weren't any. At least to date he hadn't discovered any.

Jivan stood and looked out the window. Then he turned back to Jacob. "Traditionally," he explained. "I'd just assassinate you. Get you out of the way. But we found it more effective to get rid of our problems by creating solutions. Solutions to other problems. See, a few outlaws infiltrated the Empire and murdered one our most revered heroes. Of course, citizens cannot find out about this. It would be too much to bear, and it would reveal the incompetence of the Athmans, who, as we know, though we might not both agree, are stronger than the gods and are therefore infallible."
Jacob barked. "No such caste as Athman. It's all made up. Artificial. It's all a fuckin lie!"

Jivan shook his head and shrug. He didn't really care, and tried not to think more on what Jacob had just said. "See, that's the attitude that got you in this mess in the first place." Jacob began looking around his kitchen and into the living room. It was the first time he realized all the plans and blueprints pinned up against bulletin boards. They had never been there before. They were setting him up. "Yes," Jivan smirked. "You are at home. Don't recognize it, do you? Yes, we changed some things, added others." He moved to one blueprint of a coliseum in Adhoya. He turned back to Jacob. "Unfortunately you were planning to unleash N7 at the Adhoya Kalidasa Games. Would have been devastating but the Asura Forces and the Hanuman Guard were able to prevent the atrocity. Your story will be the talk of the day, the other story, the assassination of Kulwar will be forgotten. But before I make you infamous, I will need the names of everyone involved in the train you're running, and you are running a train."

Jacob looked up at him, defiantly, and spat. In that moment Jivan swerved and smiled. Predictable. Smirking, Jivan cleared his throat and approached Jacob. "I'll get what I want. I always do." Though he knew Jacob wouldn't budge. He'd die an agonizing death ten times before he ever compromised his supporters. But Jivan played the game he loved to play. What else was there to do? He added, "We can do this the easy way, or we can do this my way, your choice."

"Fuck you!"

Jivan smiled his appreciation. "Thought you'd want to do this my way. My way's more fun." A moment later he smashed the hammer against Jacob's kneecap but not strong enough to dislodge it. Jacob screamed in agony. "I'll give you three more like that before I actually break it."

"Fuck you!"

And three more came with the last one dislodging and shattering the kneecap permanently. Jivan didn't even flinch. All he saw in his mind's eye was his wife and boy, and how outlaws had butchered them all. His sympathy, his empathy, along with most of his physical body had died with them that faithful night. Now there was only hate on top of hate on top of hate. Every interrogation was a small release from a casket that was ready to explode. Without emotion or expression, Jivan watched Jacob sob and grovel. When his groveling subsided, he pulled out a small pen. "Not a pen," he said, showcasing what was a RAD standard issue zapper. "Standard issue for RAD, and yes we do exist." No one could confirm or deny the existence of RAD. But the outlaws were certain they did exist and that some RAD agents had even infiltrated outlaw bands posing as outlaws. "You'd be surprised how much of a jolt this thing's got. One jolt knocks a person out for hours. I have it on a different setting though. Slow-fry. For interrogations just like these. If you force me to use it long enough, I promise you, it will fry you inside out." He waited for a response he never got. "Everyone in the train. I want to know who helps them remove the chip, who helps them escape their master, what's the first safe-house, the next, the next, how are you suspending animation so as to be able to pass gate security and move slaves into the Deadlands."

Jacob closed his eyes.

Jivan laughed. "No?"

Jacob shook his head.

Jivan smiled and zapped him. Jacob shook violently and cried out in pain. When Jacob finally recovered, Jivan asked, "How about now?" He didn't have to ask. Jacob would stay true till the end. But Jivan knew he couldn't kill him. He needed to deliver him to the Athmans. He zapped him again. Again he waited for him to recover. "How about now?" And Jacob continued to shake his head defiantly. With a pleased nod, Jivan grabbed a jar off the table next to the other tools of torture. G9 adrenal larvae. Thin like thread, and shorter than maggots, they entered the ears or nose and fed off the brain.

Jivan slowly and deliberately opened the jar and pulled out a maggot with tweezers and dangled it in front of Jacob. Jacob knew exactly what it was. Jivan continued:

"I find these guys really effective when I can't directly kill someone. Which, by the way, is the situation I'm in now. Afraid it's true. I do need you alive and I think you know that. But the thing is you can place these bioweapons in the nose or ear and they squirm their way to the brain for an adrenalin feast that could last up to a week or a month until they hatch into butterflies. I swear whoever thought these guys was sick. Truly sick. You're alive the whole while and the headaches grow stronger and stronger until you want to blow your own head off. But you can't. You really can't. You want to know why you can't. Not because you're scared, but because this little bugger is smart. The first thing he latches on to is your control center. You can't do anything it doesn't want you to do until it morphs and breaks out of your head like a cocoon. Second thing he does is he roots his way to is your adrenal glands. Headaches and rage. You can imagine what these guys did to the enemy. Got them killing each other to satisfy his unquenchable appetite for adrenalin. Entire platoons of adrenalin junkies tore each other to bits and pieces because of these little guys. Hard to imagine, but true. I've seen pictures. This is some evil shit. Beautiful, but evil. I've experimented with them and this is what I discovered. They don't need to enter through the nose or ears. Surprised me, but they don't. If I place this guy on your foot, he'll burrow through your toe and squirm his way to your head. Very long, very painful." Jivan motioned to Harun. Harun stood, then made his way to Jacob. A moment later he pulled off Jacob's shoe. "Once this little guy begins his journey toward his sacred food that will turn him into a butterfly it's too late. There is no way of stopping him."

Jacob closed his eyes. "Please," he said. "You don't have to do this." A tear slipped down his face as he waited for the inevitable.

"But I do," Jivan answered. "I really do." And he meant every word.

"You're not a murderer."

"Thanks, Jacob. I really appreciate that, and you're right. I'm not a murderer. You're right because you, Jacob Varma, are not a fuckin person. You're not. You ceased being a person the day you turned your back on the Athmans. You, like the salves you help, are lechers...Lechers are nothing more than pests. What I am Jacob, is a fuckin exterminator."

"You're not...Jivan...you're not..."
Jivan started. His eyes widened. "How did you know my name?" There was a mole in the agency. "What do you know about me?"

"I know who you are, and you are not a murderer." Jivan placed the G9 on his foot. "You're right I'm not." He watched the G9 begin to burrow through the top of Jacob's toe. "I can intervene now...but once he's in..."

"One day you will regret this."

"No I won't. Never. There is nothing to regret."

"When you do, know that I forgive you."

"You forgive me!" He looked to Harun and Shera. Both shrugged. Then he turned back to Jacob. "Who are you to forgive me lecher!"

He turned in anger to Shera. "You have enough for a voice print?" He asked, knowing once the G9 began making its way up to his brain it would be over.
Shera nodded. She had more than enough to fabricate a false confession.

"Good!" Jivan instantly thrust his fist into Jacobs mouth, grabbed his tongue, pulled it out and sliced it deep. Not enough to severe it, just enough to silence him. Then he stepped backed and waited for the G9 to do its good work. When Jacob began shifting in his seat, then squirming and agonizing, he turned to Harun and Shera and told them to prepare the footage and confession as he swept his home for intel on the train he was running. They nodded and Jivan proceeded to search the home. After an hour or so he found a small safe in Jacob's bedroom. When he hacked it open he found and file with pictures of him. His cover was blown. Sympathizers and rebels knew his identity. Embedded in the pictures he found an old weathered and half-burned picture of him and his family from his old life. He took a moment to remember his son Jaylum and his wife Sahiba. Red hate gathered in his heart. Suddenly, with wet eyes, he quit the room, surged down the stairs, and kicked Jacob to the ground.

Shera and Harun stared at one another. They had never seen Jivan so out of his element.

Instantly Jivan lifted Jacob back up and demanded to know why he had an entire file on him and his family. Jacob tried to answer, but nothing came out, save a gurgle of saliva and blood that sputtered in this direction and that. It was no use. Then, as the G9 squirmed up the neck and through veins in the cheek, Jacob screamed in terrible agony and Jivan knew it was all over now; Jacob was finished, and he would never know who the mole was or why sympathizers and outlaws were tracking him.

Jacob screamed and begged for a quick death that never came as the man-made parasite began to plant its roots in his adrenal glands and feast. In the living room, Jivan and his agents ignored him as they typed in a confession in a computer pad and edited a story about an Athman-Aryan who had turned his back against the Divine Society and wanted to free the untouchables. Above the agonizing screams in the background, they listened:

"We are a bored people...we aren't tyrannized by the threat of too little, we are tyrannized by too much. Having too much is sometimes more oppressive than having too little. Look at what we've become. Bongs to go torture people as entertainment. Coliseums like the Roman times. People using genetic modifiers to look like animals. Drugs aren't even good enough anymore to feel...to feel anything we must relive the deaths of gladiators and outlaws. Kalima is the most inhumane drug known to man! Yet we revere our Kalima designers, our Kalidasa more than actors and singers. More than teachers and professionals! What has become of us! We have entered the age of Kali and the Athmans are responsible for all the darkness and despair. Athmans who use violence to keep us distracted and entertained so that we don't look to what the outlaws are trying to say, or question the history that says the divine hierarchy is a lie. Caste and jati is a lie! And the greatest lie that says the Athmans have always been the natural rulers of society. It's not true. It's all cooked up. There was no such caste as the Athmans before the Collapse. The Purge was their last step in erasing and reinventing history. We need to wake up. Society as it was! Society as it was! Free and interdependent castes! Not slaves and masters! Christianity as it was! Judaism as it was! Islam as it was! Free! Free and without the lies of the Athman!"

Harun stopped the confession. "Good?" he asked. "I actually found most of this shit from one of his diary entries.

"Good enough," Jivan said flatly. "But take out the last part. Take out any reference to the Athmans. Make it about something else. It's always about something else. We don't want people thinking about the Athmans or caste."

"What should I change it to?"

"I don't know," Jivan shrugged. "Make it more about separatism. Make it about a group of separatists who want to break away from Aryana."

"No one will believe it."
Jivan scoffed. "They will believe it. They will believe what we tell them to believe. Who will say or report otherwise?"

Harun smirked.
Shera nodded in agreement. She grabbed the pad from Harun, typed something in, then played an altered version of the confession in Jacob's voice:

"...We believe we are unique and we believe we need our own nation. We tried to negotiate but all has failed and now we have no choice but to turn to drastic measures. I am sorry so many had to die, but I assure you many more will die until we get our own land and empire."

Jivan nodded. "Good. But give them a name or make up some new cult or religion. It will make them sound more legit, and it will give our bored citizens something to fear and talk about. Make it something new. A religion nobody has ever heard about." While saying this, he pulled out a needle to collect Jacob's brain fluids. He added: "The key is that we never direct attention toward caste. It's always something else. We don't want anyone poking their nose in the past, or trying to investigate the origins and nature of the Divine Society."

"Got it," Shera said.
Harun nodded.

"Just send me the final cut and I'll send it off." Jivan said as he quit the living room and entered the kitchen to find Jacob sprawled over the floor in a puddle of his own sweat and blood. With slow, meditative movements, Jivan pierced the back of his head with the needle, drew some spinal fluid, then pulled out the needle. He always collected the memories of his victims. He didn't know why. He still hadn't brought them to a Kalidasa to transform them into Kalima, but one day he would. When he was old and bored and needed some excitement he would relive his life through the eyes of his victims. It was a fun thought. To see himself young again, and to experience himself from another point of view. The marvels of Aryan science and technology. He was living in the greatest age of all even if the outlaws were right when they said that they were living in the age of kali. He couldn't imagine any other age or any other society. Anything else was simply primitive, boring and uncivilized. Then, placing the needle in a hidden pocket in his jacket, he turned his back on the withering fool who would dare sin against the Athmans, and made way his way outside, sending Zaraz Keel a quick thought-message through his S-I that he would have his news piece as promised for the morning news. Zaraz sent him back a smiling yellow icon which only Jivan could see and that vaporized just as soon as it appeared.

Jivan then entered his t-rax and drove the rest of the night around the empire searching for trouble without finding any. He rarely slept. He preferred not to sleep. For in his dreams his family and friends were still alive, and in his dreams they felt so real he never wanted to wake up. And sometimes, the dreams turned to nightmares, and his friends and family were outlaws attacking and sabotaging the empire. Those were strange dreams. Strange dreams, indeed.

Just as the sun began to rise above the wall, Jivan stopped the t-rax in midair. Slowly the vehicle descended to the ground with a soft hiss. When he was parked he shut the engine and closed his eyes, remembering. After a while he opened his eyes to watch the crimson sun rise over the wall, wondering if in death he would see them again. Then he reached over to the passenger seat and grabbed the file Jacob Varma had been keeping on him. He opened it and began to peruse the pages. Pictures. Contacts. Blueprints. Blueprints of the Aryan technology running through his veins.

How did Jacob know he was a RAD agent? Who had given him up to the outlaws? Why did they want to know what kind of humanoid technology was in him? Was his life in danger? He didn't really care. Death would be relief. The only thing that he did care about was dying before he had found the man who had engineered his demise. Jivan had personally butchered the outlaws responsible for killing his friends and family but not the one who had planned it all. He would. It was just a matter of time. And as he thought this the sun came over the Wall, the night lights faded one by one, and all the massive tele-screens embedded in the Wall and all the massive screens overlooking the streets like billboards buzzed suddenly to life with the empire's official news channel, Channel One, or the All Aryan News Channel, which would play the news story of the day on a loop until two or three in the morning so that each citizen would have been properly stuffed with all the arguments and buzz words and euphemisms and opinions that emphasized, supported and reinforced Aryan-Athman interests.

Throughout the empire the news played with pictures of Jacob Varma next to canisters of N7 along with footage of Jacob leading an outfit of slaves in prayer:

[A picture of General, then a montage of his best moments on his reality show]

Today in the news, General Gill, Kashtriya-Sikh, dies of natural causes after a lifetime devoted to the protection and defense of Aryan-Athman Society.

[Suddenly the images flashed and changed to images of Jacob Varma]

Lawyer Jacob Varma caught with N7 and confesses to leading a separatist movement led by Brahman and Sudra slaves. These Nirataaru separatists feel they should have their own country and want to take half the empire with them. Top agents have secured alarming confessions of these treasonists including the confession of their leader Varma. Today we will explore the Nirataaru religion which was created by Varma and how he was planning to murder thousands of citizens to force the peaceful and non-violent Athmans into giving him his own empire.

[A montage of fabricated footage of Varma confessing]

Jivan immediately recognized Harun and Shera's good work. He laughed. Job well done! Bloody well done! Bloody citizens would believe anything so long as the television made it seem and feel official. Anything that played on those massive screens and that was described as a 'news story' was swallowed without thought or question. The more news they stuffed citizens with the less they knew. It was wonderful.

A sudden chime.

Jivan answered his S-I. Biopixels began to form into a short document before his eyes that only he could see. It was General Kulwar Patwa Singh Gill's official obituary. He read:

General Kulwar Patwa Singh Gill
6/17/2034 - 8/7/2111
Ludhiana District
Kashtriya

Kulwar Patwa Singh Gill, former General of the Empire, beloved TV personality and founder of the Niran-Kali Sikhs devoted to the protection of the Athman caste and who built a sprawling golden statue of Athma for his followers to worship died on 7th August 2111 in his palace. He was 77. The cause was heart failure, his physician, Aftab Kumar, said. Kulwar served twice as the Director of the Asura Security Forces and once as General of the Empire before he became host to various reality shows devoted to capturing wanted Outlaws in the Deadlands. Many credit the General with having brought the Outlaw insurgency under control and for being the one who returned peace and stability to the Empire. He is known to be an uncompromising General with unsurpassed interrogation techniques. He helped invent many of the methods used by security forces to secure difficult information from captured Outlaws. He was also instrumental in legalizing Kalima for officers in order to help them navigate the memories of deceased Outlaws for counter-insurgence intelligence. Later Kulwar helped legalize Kalima for the higher castes. He later sold the memories of Outlaws he exterminated on TV at a premium. To this day his Kalima is the most sought after designer drug in the Empire. He served the Athmans with great honor and dignity. He took the war against the Outlaws to another level. Many believe he will be born an Athman in the next life for his deeds in this life. Athmanu held on the 13th August 2111.